Love You Until...

By Lisa McCourt

Illustrated by William Haines

Paulist Press

New York/Mahwah, N.J.

Jacket design by William Haines

Text copyright © 1999 by Lisa McCourt

Illustrations copyright © 1999 by William Haines

Library of Congress Cataloging-in-Publication Data

McCourt, Lisa
    Love you until- -/ by Lisa McCourt ; illustrated by William
Haines.
        p.   cm.
    Summary: Mama and Mike take turns saying that they will
love each other until a fish rides a bike, the mountains go flat, and
marshmallows grow on a tree.
    ISBN 0-8091-6658-5 (alk. paper)
    [1. Love--Fiction. 2. Mother and child--Fiction. 3. Stories in
rhyme.] I. Haines, William, ill. II Title.
PZ8.3.M45947Lo 1999
[E]--dc21
                                                        98-32045
                                                          CIP
                                                          AC

Published by Paulist Press
997 Macarthur Boulevard
Mahwah, New Jersey 07430
www.paulistpress.com

Printed and bound in Mexico

For Tucker, and for all my Mama-friends and their forever-and-ever loved ones.
–LM

For my grandkids Teryn, Christian, Brandon, Tyler, Tennille, Sean, Tamara, Austin,
Evan, Tim, Jamie, Carly and Riley.
–WH

One day Mama said to Mike,
"I'll love you until a fish rides a bike!"

"I know," said Mike, "and I can beat that.
I will love *you* till the mountains go flat!"

"Oh no," said Mama, "you can't beat me...
I'll love you till marshmallows grow on a tree!"

Mike said, "That's a
really long time,
but I will love *you*
until two equals nine!"

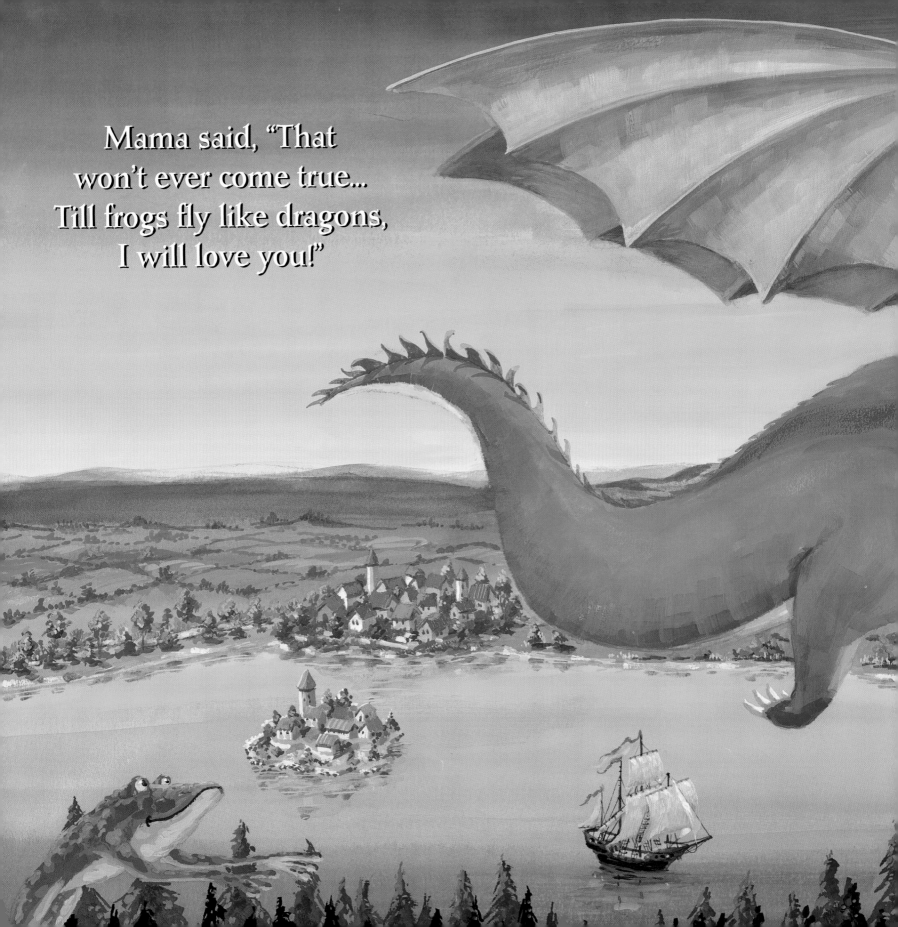

Mama said, "That
won't ever come true...
Till frogs fly like dragons,
I will love you!"

Mike said to Mama,
"That's not so weird.
I will love *you* till
Aunt Jane grows a beard!"

"I'll love you," said Mama,
"till stars in the sky
float down here to Earth
to eat pizza pie!"

"I will love *you* even longer than that--

I'll love you till Boris turns into a cat!"

"I'll love you," said Mama, "until our whole street

"Oh, Mama," laughed Mike,
"you know that can't be.
I'll love you till purple hair
grows from my knee!"

Mama said, "I've got
a silly one, too--
I will love *you* till
bananas turn blue!"

"I'll love you," Mike said, as he giggled and danced, "till an orange rhinoceros borrows my pants!"

"I'll love you," said Mama,
"till we need a horn
to call home our
naughty new pet unicorn!"

"I'll love you till elephants wear striped pajamas,

and turkeys go bowling,

and bears ride on llamas,

and ants are as big as
the truck Papa drives,

and bees live in oceans
and fish live in hives,

and porcupines all have
soft, silky fur,

and cats bark and growl
and dogs only purr,

and..." "WAIT!" Mama shouted,
"I can't top this!
As much as I love you,
you've made the best list!"

She squeezed Mike
and ruffled the hair on his head.
"I'll love you
forever and ever," she said.